StarFriends

SECRET SPELL

To Spike, who gives me so
many amazing ideas!—L.C.

To Katie—L.F.

tiger tales

5 River Road, Suite 128, Wilton, CT 06897
Published in the United States 2020
Originally published in Great Britain 2018
by the Little Tiger Group
Text copyright © 2018 Linda Chapman
Illustrations copyright © 2018 Lucy Fleming
ISBN-13: 978-1-68010-468-4
ISBN-10: 1-68010-468-3
Printed in the USA
STP/4800/0347/0620
2 4 6 8 10 9 7 5 3 1

For more insight and activities,
visit us at www.tigertalesbooks.com

Star Friends

Secret Spell

BY LINDA CHAPMAN

ILLUSTRATED BY LUCY FLEMING

tiger tales

Contents

1
IN THE STAR WORLD

A snowy owl, a badger, a stag, and a wolf gathered by a waterfall of falling stars. Their fur and feathers glittered with stardust, and their eyes were a deep indigo blue. The owl hooted softly. "My friends, let us see what is happening with the young animals and their Star Friends in the human world."

As he touched the surface of the pool with the tip of his wing, an image slowly formed. Four girls and four animals with indigo eyes were settling down for the night. A girl with

dark-blond hair was hugging a fox, a girl with black curls was cuddling a red squirrel, a girl with long dark brown hair was petting a deer, and a girl with red hair was curled up beside a wildcat with a tabby coat.

"They all look happy," said the badger with a sigh of relief.

Hunter the owl nodded. "The young animals are doing well. They have been teaching their Star Friends how to use magic to keep the human world safe. The good deeds they have done so far have strengthened the magic current that flows between our world and the human world, and has made their magical abilities stronger."

The wolf stiffened. "The picture is changing!"

A new image formed, showing a person wearing a black hooded robe and holding a stone bowl filled with small objects. Shadows were swirling up from the ground.

The stag pawed the earth in alarm. "Someone is working dark magic near the Star Friends!"

The owl nodded gravely. "I'm afraid it appears to be as we suspected. Two Shades have already been defeated by the Star Animals and their friends. But now more trouble is coming their way."

The wolf growled. "I believe I know this

person we can see."

"You do, my friend," said the owl. "She has caused problems in the past. Her magic was once bound, but now she is able to use it again."

"What can we do to stop her?" said the stag.

"Nothing." The owl shook his head. "It is up to the new Star Animals and their friends to stop this threat. All we can do is watch."

"And hope the dark magic does not win," said the wolf grimly.

2
A Terrible Dream

Mia stood on a bridge. On one side, a dark mist rose from the ground. Mia's blood turned to ice as the mist took the shape of a tall, thin figure. It was a Shade—an evil spirit from the shadows who liked to hurt people.

As the Shade fixed its eyes on her, Mia looked around desperately. Where was Bracken, her Star Animal? And where were her friends and their Star Animals?

"Let me past!" the Shade hissed.

Mia stood her ground. "No!"

In a shimmer of starlight, a fox with indigo eyes appeared beside her.

"Bracken!" Mia whispered in relief.

Bracken leaped between Mia and the Shade. "Go back to the shadows!" he growled.

The Shade snickered. "Why should we listen to you? Only a Spirit Speaker can command us."

Mia's heart skipped a beat as more dark shapes started to form behind the first Shade.

They spoke with one eerie voice. "You may have defeated the Wish Shade, but the one using dark magic has conjured more of us. She wants us to make all your fears come true!"

Stepping forward, the first Shade swiped at Bracken, who yelped in pain as sharp nails scratched him.

"Bracken!" Mia screamed.

Mia felt something licking her nose.

"I'm here, Mia."

Hearing Bracken's voice, she blinked open her eyes and looked into his anxious face. Then she felt a hand on her shoulder and heard Sita gently saying, "Mia, wake up."

Mia's heart gradually slowed. She was in her bedroom with Bracken on her lap and Sita kneeling beside her. Sita's Star Animal, a gentle deer named Willow, was next to Sita, while Lexi and Violet were still fast asleep on the floor nearby with their Star Animals—a red squirrel and a wildcat. The gray light of dawn was just streaking across the sky.

"Were you having a bad dream?" Sita whispered.

Mia nodded. "It was about a Shade." She shivered as she remembered. "A lot of Shades. Bracken got hurt. It was horrible."

Bracken licked her hand, and Mia wrapped her arms around him. She couldn't bear the thought of Bracken being injured. Ever since they had become Star Friends a few weeks ago, she had felt a deep bond with him—she loved him more than anything in the world.

It's like he's part of me, she realized.

The day she had met him in a clearing in the woods was etched into her mind. To Mia's amazement, he had talked to her, telling her he was from a different world and that if she wanted to be his Star Friend, he would teach her how to use magic to do good and make the world a better place. Most importantly of all, they had to stop anyone who was trying to use dark magic to hurt others. It had been even more amazing when her best friends had become Star Friends, too.

"You probably had a nightmare because of that horrible Wish Shade we fought last night," Sita said. "But Violet sent it back to the shadows, remember? It's gone. There's nothing to worry about."

As Mia felt her fear fade, she wondered if Sita was using her special magic abilities. The Star Animals had taught them all how to use the magic current that flowed between the human world and the Star World. The girls had found they each had different skills. Mia could see things that were happening elsewhere and look into the future; Sita could heal and soothe; Lexi was amazingly agile; and Violet could shadow-travel. Not only that, Violet was also a Spirit Speaker, which meant she could command Shades and send them back to the shadows.

Mia gave Sita a grateful look. "You're right. I'm sorry I woke you up."

"Mia, what did you see?" Bracken asked.

"Does it matter?" Sita said. "It was just a dream."

Bracken looked anxious. "I'm not sure. As Mia's magic sight abilities get stronger, there might be things in her dreams that come true."

Mia felt a flicker of alarm and tried to remember. "I was on a bridge, and the Shade said something about the one who had conjured the Wish Shade calling more Shades … and then more of them appeared. Then the Shade attacked."

"I hope it doesn't come true," said Sita. "It was scary enough facing just one Shade last night. I don't want to have to fight a bunch of them."

Just then, Violet sat up sleepily and pushed her red hair out of her face. "What's going on?"

Beside her, Sorrel the wildcat stretched and rolled onto her back. "I refuse to believe it's morning yet," she yawned. "Whatever it is, it can wait."

"No, it can't. This could be important. Wakey-wakey, pussycat," said Bracken, jumping over Sorrel's tummy and landing on the end of her fluffy tail. "We all need to talk."

The wildcat leaped to her feet and hissed. But Bracken ignored her and trotted over to wake Juniper the squirrel and Lexi, who were curled up together inside Lexi's sleeping bag. Juniper squeaked in protest and snuggled closer into Lexi's arms, so Bracken kept licking them both until they woke up.

Soon the girls were all sitting around in a circle, cuddling their animals.

"If Bracken's right and Mia's dream *is* true," said Violet, "then we have to try and find out who is conjuring these Shades."

"The Shade said it was a woman," Mia remembered. "And that she's the same person who conjured the Wish Shade."

"I wish we could use your magic to find out more, Mia," said Lexi.

Mia wished that, too, but she had already tried to see who had conjured the Wish Shade, and her magic had shown her nothing but darkness. Bracken had told her it seemed as though the person was using a spell to conceal herself.

"We should start by finding out who gave the little garden gnome with the Wish Shade trapped inside to Paige's family," said Violet. "We need to know if that person knew about the Wish Shade and that it was going to make wishes come true in a horrible way."

Mia nodded. "I asked Paige once, and she said

that the gnome was from a friend of her mom's. We need to find out her name." She jumped to her feet. "Let's go to Paige's house now."

Violet leaped up, too. "Yes, let's!"

"Wait!" said Lexi. "Everyone will still be in bed."

"Oh, yeah," said Violet, looking disappointed.

Mia sighed. Now that they had a plan, she wanted to act on it right away.

"While we're waiting, you could all try doing some magic," Bracken said. "Mia's magic seems to have gotten stronger from defeating the Shade yesterday, so maybe everyone else's will have, too."

Juniper jumped onto Mia's desk, his tail curling behind him. "You might all be able to do new things!"

"Oh, I hope so! I can already do so many cool things with my magic. Imagine if I could do even more," said Violet.

Mia saw Lexi roll her eyes. Violet sometimes

said things that made her sound boastful, and it really irritated Lexi. It used to annoy Mia, too, but now Mia was beginning to think that Violet didn't mean to show off; she just didn't always think about how what she said would sound to other people.

"We could go to the clearing," said Willow.

Bracken yapped in agreement, Juniper chattered happily, and Sorrel nodded her head. The animals all loved the clearing in the woods. It was where they had first appeared when they had traveled from the Star World, and it was an especially magical place.

Juniper leaped onto Lexi's shoulder. "When we're at the clearing, we might also find out which of you is the super-strong one the Wish Shade spoke about."

Mia felt a jolt run through her. Just before the Wish Shade had been sent back to the shadows, it had told them that one of them would turn out to be incredibly powerful—

so powerful that the person using dark magic would be scared of them.

"I'd forgotten about that," said Sita.

"Me, too," said Lexi.

"It's obviously going to be Violet," declared Sorrel. "She can shadow-travel and command Shades already."

Violet looked happy.

"It might not be Violet," protested Lexi. "It could be Mia or Sita."

"Oh, I don't want it to be me," said Sita hurriedly. "I'm happy just healing people."

"It could be you, Lexi," Mia put in. "Your agility is incredible. I wish I could run and jump and climb like you."

Bracken put his paws up on Mia's leg. "I bet you're the special one, Mia," he whispered.

Mia hugged him. She really hoped so!

Sorrel trotted to the door, her tail ramrod straight. "Why are you all standing around talking?" she said. "Let's go!"

3
A Little Magic Practice

The girls pulled on their clothes. As they left Mia's bedroom, the animals vanished—it was important for them to stay secret from other humans.

Violet fell into step beside Mia as they went downstairs. "This is really exciting, isn't it?" she said in a low voice. "We might all have new powers. And it sounds like there will be more Shades for us to fight."

Mia nodded in agreement. Although Shades were scary, she felt a thrill at the thought of

using her magic to stop
them. "Last night was
exciting, wasn't it?" she
said to Violet.

Violet grinned.
"Chasing a possessed
gnome, rescuing friends
from a burning shed,
and using magic to fight
an evil Shade…. I mean,
who'd want to do anything
else on a Saturday evening!"

Glancing at Violet's happy
face, Mia remembered something
Sita had said—that she thought Violet had been
lonely and was really enjoying hanging around
with them now that they were all Star Friends.
Mia was beginning to feel Sita was right.

When they went into the kitchen, they
found Mia's little brother, Alex, sitting in his
high chair.

"Morning, girls!" Mr. Greene said cheerfully. "Nice to see you up so bright and early."

"We were going to go out for a bike ride," Mia said.

"Okay, but have some breakfast first."

"Bek-fast!" called Alex, offering his sister a piece of his toast.

Mia grinned. "Thanks, Alex, but I'll get my own."

Alex threw the toast on the floor. "All gone." He giggled.

"Come on, young man," Mr. Greene said, undoing the harness and scooping Alex up out of the high chair. "We're going to rake some leaves in the yard together."

Alex shook his head firmly. "No leaves. No beetles."

"Don't be silly. Beetles won't hurt you," his dad said.

"No beetles! No!" Alex's voice rose, and he struggled in his dad's arms.

"He's scared of beetles," Mia explained to the others as they got out the cereal boxes. "He was helping Dad the other day, and they found a nest of beetles under a pile of leaves."

"All right, Alex, all right," Mr. Greene said soothingly. "You can play in the sandbox then."

Alex continued to struggle. "No yard! No!"

Sita went over and took his hands in hers. "Oh, Alex, don't worry. The beetles will leave you alone. You can have a nice time playing in the sandbox." Alex stopped wriggling and stared at her as she spoke. "You can play with your shovel, can't you?" Sita went on, her gentle brown eyes fixed on his.

"Play," Alex repeated, gazing at her. Then he looked up at his dad. "Me play outside."

Mr. Greene blinked. "Okay, great." He turned to Sita. "You really have a knack with little ones, Sita."

Sita smiled. "I get a lot of practice with my little brother."

Mr. Greene nodded. "Well, thanks," he said, and he carried Alex outside.

"Were you using your magic then?" Mia whispered to Sita.

She nodded and grinned. "Of course. Willow told me we should use it as often as we can to help people. Every bit of good we do strengthens the magic current."

"And our own magical abilities," added Violet.

They had just started to eat breakfast when Mr. Greene came back in.

"Mia, you haven't seen the key for the shed, have you?"

Mia shook her head. "I'm sorry, no."

Mr. Greene frowned then went out again, muttering, "I don't know where it could be."

Mia thought for a second and then, remembering what Sita had said about using their magic to help people as much as they could, she picked up a spoon. Could she find the key? She turned over the spoon and looked into the shiny surface, opening her mind to the current of magic. She felt it flow into her, making her tingle all over.

"Show me the key to the shed," she whispered.

An image formed in the back of the spoon. It showed a key inside an old pottery vase. Mia recognized it as one of the flowerpots that sat just under the shelf where the key was usually kept. The key must have fallen into the vase!

She put down the spoon and hurried to the back door.

"Dad!" Her dad was looking under the jam jars and paint cans. "Have you looked in the flowerpots? It might have fallen off the shelf."

"I did take a quick look," Mr. Greene said.

Mia's eyes fell on the vase, and she picked it up and turned it upside down. A metal key dropped out. "It's here! Look!"

"Oh, great job!" her dad said. "That was a lucky guess."

"Yep," Mia said, hiding her smile. Being able to do magic was awesome!

✦ ✦ ✦

As soon as they had put away their bowls, the girls set off on their bikes. It was a crisp November morning, and the sun was just starting to rise. The chilly breeze made their cheeks glow, and Mia was glad she had put on her scarf and gloves. The streets of Westport had an early Sunday morning quietness about them. A few people were out walking dogs or running, but most of the houses still had their curtains drawn. The girls passed the playing fields where a huge bonfire was prepared.

"Are you all going to the fireworks tonight?" Mia asked as they rode past.

Her friends nodded.

"How about we meet there at six?" Sita suggested.

"I can't be there until six fifteen," said Lexi. "Can we meet then? I'll be with my math tutor until six."

Violet frowned. "Math tutor? Why do you have a math tutor? You're almost as good at math as me."

Mia groaned inwardly. Couldn't Violet tell that saying things like that would really irritate Lexi?

"Because I'm taking an entrance exam for high school in January, and my mom wants me to try and get a scholarship," Lexi retorted. "And actually I'm *just* as good at math as you!"

"Oh, look, there's Aunt Carol's house," Mia said hurriedly before Violet could reply. "Maybe we should stop by later and tell her what happened last night."

Aunt Carol was an elderly lady who could do magic—not with a Star Animal, but by using crystals. She had been one of Mia's grandmother's best friends, but Grandma Anne had died just a few months ago. Aunt Carol had told Mia that she knew all about Star Animals because she had seen Grandma Anne's Star Animal—a wolf—when they were children. Aunt Carol had said that she and Grandma Anne used to do magic together, and now she wanted to help Mia and her friends. Bracken and the other Star Animals weren't too sure about having the help of someone who wasn't a Star Friend, but Mia really liked being able to talk to Aunt Carol about magic and ask for her advice.

"Should we see if she's home now?" Violet asked.

"It's still pretty early," said Mia. "I'll see her later."

The girls rode across the main road and headed onto the track that led down through the wooded valley to the beach. Seagulls swooped overhead, and they could hear the distant sound of the ocean. The path to the clearing was halfway down the track, opposite Grandma Anne's house.

The girls left their bikes in the front yard. The house was empty now—Mia's parents had gradually been clearing out all her grandma's things. Brambles caught at their legs as they pushed their way along the overgrown path, and the air smelled of fallen leaves and dampness.

Emerging into the clearing, they called their animals' names. The four Star Animals appeared instantly. Bracken jumped around Mia, yapping excitedly. Juniper scampered up a tree. Willow cantered here and there, making playful little leaps, and Sorrel rubbed against Violet's legs, purring loudly.

Mia kneeled down and Bracken jumped onto her lap, licking her cheeks and snuffling at her ears. She hugged his warm body. "It's magic time," she told him.

"I wonder if you'll be able to do anything new," he said.

Mia grinned and pulled a small mirror out

of her pocket. "Only one way to find out. I'm going to try looking into the past." It was something she had tried to do before but had never managed.

Violet overheard. "Remember to relax!" she called.

"I will, thanks," Mia said gratefully. When she'd been struggling with her magic the week before, Violet had given Mia some tips that had really worked.

Mia remembered Violet's advice as she looked into the mirror. Breathe in for five seconds, hold her breath for five seconds, breathe out. Do that again and again. Count backward from ten. She felt a sense of calm settle over her. Bracken snuggled against her legs and Mia stared at the mirror, letting everything else fade away....

The surface of the mirror shimmered. What did she want to see?

"Show me Grandma Anne," she breathed. "Show me her with her Star Animal."

To her excitement, an image appeared in
the mirror's surface. It was a young teenager
dressed in old-fashioned clothes—
brown pants tucked into socks
and sturdy shoes, a brown
V-neck sweater, and
blond hair held back
by a scarf. It was
Grandma Anne!
Mia recognized her
grandmother from old
photos she had seen.
Grandma Anne was
in the woods, and a slim
silver wolf with indigo eyes
was at her side. One of her hands
was resting on the wolf's back, and in the other
she held a small mirror. Mia caught her breath.
It was the same mirror she was holding now—
Grandma Anne had given it to her a year ago.

Her fingers tightened as she wondered if her

grandmother had suspected that she was also going to be a Star Friend. She'd talked to her so often about magic. Warmth flooded through her as she imagined how happy her grandma would be if she knew that Mia *was* a Star Friend now.

She let the image fade.

"Did you see your grandmother?" Bracken asked eagerly.

"Yes," she said. "She was with her Star Animal."

Bracken jumped around her. "This is great, Mia. Your magic really *has* got stronger!"

Mia looked around, wondering what the others were doing. Sita was talking to Willow, Lexi seemed to have vanished, and Violet was standing in front of…. Mia frowned. A table? What was a table doing in the clearing? It had a faint glowing outline.

"Violet!" she called.

Violet glanced over, but before Mia could say anything, she felt a hand tug her hair. She jumped. Lexi was standing behind her.

Mia blinked. "How did you get there?"

"I can run so fast I'm invisible," Lexi said
with a grin.

Mia gaped. "That's awesome!"

"I would hardly describe it as *awesome*,"
Sorrel commented with a dismissive flick of
her tail. "In my opinion, the ability to run fast
has only limited uses."

"Oh, really," said Lexi. She leaped forward
and disappeared. Two seconds later, Lexi was
standing beside her again, and Violet was
patting the side of her head in confusion. Lexi
held out her hand to Mia. In her palm was
Violet's hair clip. "I think being able to run fast
has a lot of uses," Lexi said.

The table vanished. Sorrel hissed at Lexi.
"You made Violet lose her concentration."

"What was she trying to do?" Mia asked.
"Why was there a table there?"

"She was casting a glamour," said Bracken,

bounding over to where Violet was standing.

"Correct!" said Sorrel smugly. "Now that is *definitely* an awesome ability."

"What's a glamour?" Mia asked.

Sorrel sighed. "A glamour is when magic is used to create an illusion. Something appears, but really there's nothing there."

"A glamour can also disguise something," added Juniper.

Violet's eyes shone. "I hadn't been able to do it when I'd tried before, but now I can! Look!" She concentrated again, and a chair appeared.

"That looks so real," breathed Sita. "That's an amazing power, Violet."

Violet looked delighted.

"It is, although the glowing light makes it just a little bit obvious that it's an illusion," Mia pointed out.

"What glowing light?" said Sita, looking surprised.

Bracken nudged Mia's hand with his nose. "Mia, I think you can see the light because your magic abilities have to do with sight. To everyone else, it looks like a normal chair."

"Oh," said Mia.

Lexi linked arms with her. "I think it's just as cool to be able to see through illusions as to make them," she said with a pointed look at Violet.

"It will be a very useful ability," Bracken agreed. "The key to shattering an illusion is to refuse to believe it's real."

Mia looked at the chair. "You're not real,"

she said. The chair vanished. "Whoops, I'm sorry, Violet!"

"It's okay. I can make it come back again," said Violet. The chair reappeared.

"I don't believe in you," Mia said. It vanished again.

Violet giggled. For a few moments, they kept making the chair appear and disappear, then Violet stopped. "I want to try something else with my magic." She went and stood near a patch of shadows and beckoned for Mia to join her. "Come here, Mia. I need your help with this."

Mia went over curiously. What was Violet planning?

"Want to try and shadow-travel together?" Violet asked.

"You can take me with you?" Mia said in surprise. Mia had seen Violet transport herself from one place to another using shadows, but it hadn't occurred to her that Violet's magic could extend to other people.

"I'm not sure … but I'd like to try!" Violet's green eyes shone. "My magic feels much stronger today." She took Mia's hand. "Just relax." She stepped into the shadows. Mia stepped with her, and the world suddenly disappeared. The next second, she was staggering slightly as everything came back into view. She blinked. They were on the other side of the clearing!

"Oh, Violet, you exceptional girl!" exclaimed Sorrel in delight.

Violet grinned. "Did you see?" she called to Sita and Lexi.

"Yes," said Lexi shortly.

"That's great, Violet," said Sita enthusiastically. She frowned slightly. "Everyone seems to have gotten new powers except me."

"Healing is a wonderful power on its own," Willow told her. "I'm sure your magic will be stronger, and you'll be able to heal bigger wounds."

"Willow's right," Violet said, going over to Sita. "And you're really good at calming people down and making them relax, too."

Sita smiled at her. "Thanks. I wouldn't want to be the one with the mega-power anyway."

"I wonder which of us it will be," said Violet thoughtfully.

"Well," Sorrel began, "as I've already said, I think—" She was interrupted by a rustle in the trees.

"Someone's coming!" said Bracken.

The animals all vanished, and the girls watched warily. Who was coming into the clearing?

4
THE STRANGER

An elderly woman hurried through the trees.
Her gray hair was cut very short, and she was
wearing a scruffy beige raincoat and green
walking shoes. She had a wicker basket covered
with an old towel on one arm.

She froze as she saw the girls. "What are you
doing here?"

The girls looked at each other, taken aback
by her sharp tone.

"Um … we just came here for a walk," said
Mia.

"Leaving litter, no doubt!" snapped the woman. She spotted an empty soda can on the ground and scooped it up. "See! I knew it!"

"That's not ours," said Mia. She'd noticed it earlier and had planned to recycle it when she got back home.

"Likely story!" snorted the woman. "You kids should go away! Stay out of these woods."

"Okay … um … we'll go then," said Mia, glancing at the others.

They backed away and hurried down the footpath.

"What a weird woman!" hissed Lexi as soon as they were out of earshot.

"I didn't like her," said Sita with a shiver.

"I've never seen her before. Maybe she's just

visiting Westport," said Mia.

Westport was a large town, but she knew most of the older people who lived there by sight.

"I think she just moved here," said Violet. "I've seen her coming out of the house next door to your Aunt Carol's a few times. The one that was for sale in the summer."

Mia's heart sank. "Well, if she has moved in, I hope we don't see much of her."

Just then Mia's phone buzzed. It was a text from her mom.

> Dad says ur all out for a bike ride. If u want a hot choc then come to the Copper Kettle at 10:15. We'll be there with Alex and Cleo. Mom xxx

It was just past 10:15 a.m. "Mom and Dad are at the Copper Kettle. If we meet them there, they'll buy us a hot chocolate. Should we go?"

The Copper Kettle was a cozy bakery on the main road. The friends left their bikes in the bike rack and headed inside. The bell jingled, and they were hit with the smell of freshly bakes cakes and warm coffee. Mia breathed in deeply. "Mmm."

Her mom and dad were sitting with Alex and Cleo, Mia's fifteen-year-old sister, at a window table. Alex was coloring, and Cleo was flipping through a celebrity magazine while Mr. and Mrs. Greene were drinking their coffees.

"Mai–Mai!" cried Alex.

Cleo glanced up briefly from her magazine before continuing to read.

"Pull up some chairs, girls," said Mr. Greene.

Mia and her friends squeezed in around the table. Mary, the Copper Kettle's cheerful owner, bustled over to meet them. She was short and plump with curly brown hair and a beaming smile.

"What can I get you, girls?"

"Four hot chocolates I think, please, Mary," said Mrs. Greene, looking at the girls, who all nodded.

"What about cake?" Mr. Greene said.

Mia and Violet asked for a slice of chocolate fudge cake each, Lexi chose a white chocolate brownie, and Sita asked for lemon drizzle cake. Soon they were sipping mugs of hot chocolate topped with whipped cream and tiny pink and white marshmallows and nibbling their cake.

"I told your mom we'd be here," Mrs.
Greene said to Lexi. "She's going to come by
and pick up you and Sita. I've got your sleeping
bags and things in the car."

Alex had finished coloring and started trying
to grab handfuls of the flyers that Mary had
displayed on the windowsill.

"Put them down, Alex," said Mr. Greene.
"Take this instead." He handed Alex a toy train,
which he took happily, throwing the flyers on
the floor.

Mia picked up the flyers. As she did, she
noticed one that she hadn't seen before. "Look,
this is for a new wildlife sanctuary," she said,
showing it to her mom.

"We could go one weekend," Mrs. Greene
suggested.

Mary overheard them. "You really should
visit the sanctuary," she said. "My sister Jenny
moved into town a month or so ago, and now
she works there. She said they have squirrels,

foxes, and badgers. They take in animals that have been injured and nurse them back to health."

"We'll definitely go," said Mia to the others, who nodded.

"I'd like to run a wildlife sanctuary when I'm older," said Sita.

"Me, too," said Mia.

"I want to work with endangered animals all over the world," said Violet.

"And I want to be a vet," said Lexi.

They talked about all the things they would do when they were older until Lexi's mom arrived.

"See you at the bonfire tonight," Mia said as Lexi and Sita put their bikes into the trunk of her car.

"Six fifteen," Lexi reminded everyone.

Mia turned to her mom and dad. "I might stop by and see Aunt Carol on the way home. Is that okay?"

"That's nice of you," her mom said. "Tell Aunt Carol I'll pop over to visit her soon."

Mia was relieved that her mom didn't want to come along—she had been hoping she would have the chance to talk to Aunt Carol alone. She and Violet got their bikes and rode down the street, then Violet went on to her house and Mia turned onto Aunt Carol's street.

Getting off her bike, Mia leaned it against the wall outside Aunt Carol's house.

A delivery man was knocking at the door of the house next to Aunt Carol's. He was carrying a large cardboard box. The front door opened, and a white dog ran out.

"Jack! Come here!" shouted a voice.

The dog only had one ear and half its tail was missing, but Mia didn't care. She loved all animals. She went to the top of the driveway to stop the dog from running out into the road and held out her hand, but the dog backed away, growling. Mia was surprised. Animals usually liked her.

"It's all right," she said to the dog. "I'm not scary."

The dog directed a volley of barks in her direction.

The delivery man gave the dog a nervous look. "He doesn't seem too friendly, does he?"

Just then Mia noticed a woman with short gray hair at the door. It was the lady from the woods!

"Stay away from my dog!" the lady snapped at Mia. "And get out of my yard!"

Mia backed away as the lady called the dog into the house and snatched the package from the delivery man, slamming the door behind her. To Mia's relief, Aunt Carol answered the front door on her first knock.

"Mia, how lovely to see you! I was just making some treats to take to the bonfire tonight. Are you all right?" she asked, looking at Mia's flustered face.

"Yes." Mia swallowed. She didn't like being shouted at.

"What's the matter?" asked Aunt Carol, ushering her in.

When Mia told her what had just happened, Aunt Carol patted her hand. "Oh, my dear, how horrible. I didn't like Mrs. Crooks the moment she moved in. She's done some very strange things. She had a large shed built in the yard and then put up a really high fence. She

hardly says a word if I see her, even though
I've asked her a few times if she wants to come
over for coffee. She's always going off into the
woods at very bizarre times, too." She shook
her head. "She's very odd."

Mia felt relieved that it wasn't only the Star
Friends who thought the elderly lady was odd.

Aunt Carol led Mia into the living room.
The surfaces were decorated with large,
shining crystals and a stone bowl that had some
glittering polished stones inside. "I'm afraid I
haven't managed to find out anything more
about this Shade that's causing all the trouble."

"Oh, you don't need to worry about that
anymore," said Mia, remembering she had
good news. "It's been sent back to the
shadows."

They sat down, and Mia told Aunt Carol
everything that had happened the night before.

"My goodness," said Aunt Carol, putting her
hand to her chest. "You all did very well. How

did you do it?"

"It was Violet," said Mia. "She's a Spirit Speaker."

"I see," said Aunt Carol thoughtfully. "Well, that's lucky for you. What about the others? You've never told me what they can do."

"Lexi has powers to do with agility, and Sita is good at healing." As Mia spoke, she felt a little uncomfortable. She knew Bracken didn't like her telling Aunt Carol things about the magic—he had been told that no one except for Star Friends should know anything.

Glancing around the room, she decided to change the subject. "Aunt Carol," she said. "How do you do magic with crystals?"

"Well, crystals and stones contain their own special energy. I hold them in my hands, and by concentrating hard, I can use it—a little like you drawing on the magic current. Different crystals and stones can do different things—some can heal, others see into the future, some will help calm an angry soul, and others bring good luck. I've spent my life figuring out how to use their power."

"Is there any other type of magic—except for Crystal Magic and Star Magic?" Mia asked curiously.

"There's dark magic, of course, when people draw power from the shadows," Aunt Carol shuddered. "I don't like even thinking about that. And some people can draw magic from plants— they gather herbs and plants and make potions." She smiled. "If you hadn't met a Star Animal,

then maybe you would have discovered how to
use magic in another way. In fact, I'm sure you
could master Crystal Magic. Here." She went
to the stone bowl and pulled out a glittering
round, pink stone from the bottom. It seemed to
glow with a faint golden light. "This is a Seeing
Stone—let's see if I'm right." She held it out.

As Mia took the pretty crystal sphere, her
fingers tingled, and she caught her breath.

Aunt Carol's eyebrows
rose. "I can see you're feeling
the magic. Seeing Stones
can be used to look into
the past. You told me
you've been trying
to do that with your
own magic. Well, try
with this. Just hold it,
concentrate on it, and
tell it what you want
to see."

It was on the tip of Mia's tongue to tell Aunt Carol that she had finally managed to see into the past, but then there was a knock on the door.

"Oh, that will be my friends from the Christmas fair committee," said Aunt Carol. "We're having a knitting party this morning to make Christmas tree decorations to sell at the fair." She nodded at the stone. "Slip that in your pocket, dear. You can keep it."

Mia put the pink stone into her pocket. "Thank you! I'd better go now."

"Are you and your friends going to the bonfire tonight?" Aunt Carol asked.

"Yes," said Mia.

"I'll see you all there, then," Aunt Carol said.

Mia followed her into the hallway, and Aunt Carol opened the door to three ladies, all with baskets of yarn and knitting needles.

"Hello, dear," said Margaret, who was tall and slim and knew Grandma Anne. "How are you?"

"Fine, thank you," Mia said.

"What are you up to today?" asked Josie, who ran the town preschool and had known Mia since she was a baby.

"Oh, a lot of different things," said Mia. "I'd better go. 'Bye, Aunt Carol!" she called hastily before the ladies invited her to stay and do some knitting!

Picking up her bike, she turned around and then froze. Two garden gnomes had appeared on either side of Mrs. Crooks's front door. Garden gnomes that looked just like the gnome that the horrible Wish Shade had been trapped in!

5
DETECTIVE MIA

Mia's heart thudded in her chest. The gnomes had rosy red cheeks, little pointed hats, and big smiles. They looked just like the gnome that the Wish Shade had been in, except one had a fishing rod and one had a rabbit in its arms. She had to investigate! Could these gnomes have Shades in them, too?

She checked that no one was around and, leaving her bike against the wall, she headed up the path. She crouched down beside them and poked them gingerly with a finger.

The front door flew open. "You again! What are you doing with my new gnomes?" said Mrs. Crooks.

"Um… I was just looking at them," Mia stammered, jumping to her feet. "They're really cute."

Mrs. Crooks's eyes narrowed. "Don't you go getting any idea about stealing them."

Mia was shocked. "I wouldn't."

"You stay away," Mrs. Crooks warned.

Mia backed up the driveway. Then, jumping on her bike, she rode away as quickly as she could. Her thoughts were spinning. What was Mrs. Crooks doing with those gnomes?

Icy fingers trailed down her spine. Could Mrs. Crooks be the person doing dark magic? Mia was so busy thinking about it that she almost didn't notice Paige bouncing on the trampoline in her front yard.

"Hi, Mia!" Paige called, waving and then turning a somersault.

Mia skidded to a halt, remembering that they had been planning on asking Paige where the Wish Shade gnome had come from. "Hi, Paige. Are you okay today?"

Paige looked puzzled. "Yes, why?"

Mia lowered her voice. "After what happened with the gnome last night?"

"The gnome? What do you mean?"

Mia realized that when the Shade had been sent back to the shadows, the magic must have made Paige forget everything about it. The same had happened to her sister, Cleo, when they had sent back the Mirror Shade. "Don't worry," she said quickly. "But um … just one thing. You know the garden gnome that used to be here?"

"Yeah." Paige looked around. "Mommy must have moved it."

"Do you know where it came from?"

Mia asked hopefully.

"One of Mommy's friends gave it to us," Paige said. "She brought it over and put it in the yard. It was a lady with gray hair…. I can't remember her name. I think it was a present to say thank you to Mommy for helping with something." She grinned. "Mommy said she'd rather have had some chocolates!"

Mia's heart beat faster. Mrs. Crooks had gray hair! "Are you sure you can't remember her name?"

Paige shook her head. "No. Why?"

"It was just that I thought I might get one like him for my dad," Mia fibbed. "If you remember the lady's name, will you let me know?"

"Yep," said Paige, starting to bounce on the trampoline again. "I will. I think Mommy said she was just a friend from town."

Mia said good-bye and continued home. Mrs. Crooks had gray hair, but Aunt Carol had said that Mrs. Crooks had turned down her invitation to join her for the knitting party. Had Mrs. Crooks given the Wish Gnome to Paige's family, or was it someone else? Maybe someone who hadn't known there was a Shade trapped inside it? Mia turned things over in her mind and rode faster. She had to get home so she could talk to Bracken. She was sure Mrs. Crooks was involved—but how?

As soon as Mia reached her bedroom, she shut the door and whispered Bracken's name. He appeared in front of her, bouncing around. Mia sat on the bed, and he jumped up beside her.

"What's been happening?" he asked. He always seemed to know when she had things that she needed to talk about.

"I saw Paige," Mia said quickly. "She can't remember the name of the person who gave the Wish Gnome to her mom, but she said it was a lady from town. Also there's an elderly lady

who has moved in next to Aunt Carol. She's odd and has a strange dog, and when I came out of Aunt Carol's house, I saw two gnomes on her doorstep—just like the Wish Gnome! Could she be the person who's doing dark magic?" Mia said.

"She might be planning to put Shades inside the gnomes," said Bracken anxiously.

"That Shade in my dream said more Shades had been called from the shadows. I'd better tell the others." Mia reached for her phone but then paused. It was too risky to send a text just in case one of their parents checked their phone. "I'll tell them tonight at the bonfire," she decided. "If only Paige could remember the name of the person who gave the gnome to her mom!"

"Maybe you could use your magic to find out," Bracken said thoughtfully. "I know it didn't work when you asked to see who trapped the Shade inside the gnome…. But how about asking it to show you who *gave* the gnome?"

"That's a great idea!" Mia said. She put her

hand in her pocket to pull out the mirror, and her fingers brushed against the round pink stone that Aunt Carol had given her. She decided not to tell Bracken about it—she had a feeling he wouldn't approve of Aunt Carol suggesting she try doing magic in other ways. Leaving the stone in her pocket, she took out the mirror.

"Show me the moment the Wish Gnome arrived at Paige's house," she whispered.

The surface swirled with light, and an image appeared in the glass. Mia peered at it eagerly. She caught sight of a figure in a long coat but then, to her disappointment, the image blurred.

"Show me who gave the Wish Gnome to Paige's family," she whispered again.

But the image stayed blurry. "It's not working today," she said to Bracken. "I can't see clearly."

He licked her cheek. "Try again later."

Mia tried again several times that day, but each time, the mirror failed to show her what she wanted to see. In the end, she had to give

up and get ready to go out
for the fireworks.

"Have fun," Bracken said,
licking her nose. "I'll see you
when you get home."

Mia hugged him, then he
vanished. As she took off her
jeans to change for the bonfire,
the Seeing Stone Aunt Carol had given her
fell out of her pocket. She picked it up. It was so
pretty. Would she be able to do magic with it?

She rubbed the stone and felt the magic in it
prickle her fingers. Maybe she could use it to see
who had given the gnome to Paige's family. What
had Aunt Carol told her she needed to do?

No. She stopped herself. It felt wrong to try
and do magic with the stone without telling
Bracken. Reluctantly, she put it down on her
desk. She would tell Bracken about it later, and
together they could decide what she should do.

6
BONFIRE NIGHT

The night was cold and frosty, and the air was full of the smell of smoke as Mia walked up to the baseball field with her family. She usually liked the smell of smoke from a fire, but now it made her think about the Wish Shade trying to burn down the shed in Paige's yard when she, Lexi, and Sita were all locked inside. Horrible pictures flashed through her mind—the Wish Shade they had fought, the gnomes outside Mrs. Crooks's house, the dream she had about more Shades coming....

She spotted Lexi, Sita, and Violet and told her mom she was going to meet them. "We need to talk," she hissed as she hurried over.

"About what?" Violet said.

Sita's eyes widened. "Did you see Paige?"

Mia nodded, but before she could say anything, she was interrupted.

"Hello, girls," Aunt Carol said. She took some boxes of sparklers out of her purse. "Mia said you'd be here, so I thought I'd bring you all a little present. There's a box each."

"Thanks, Aunt Carol," said Mia.

"I love sparklers," Violet said. "Thank you!"

"Look, the boxes have a free gift with them!" said Sita. Each box of sparklers had a little yellow stretchy man taped to it.

"Cool!" said Lexi.

Aunt Carol peered at them. "How strange. I don't remember seeing those when I bought them."

Lexi took the little man off her box and waggled its legs and arms. "Do you remember the craze at school when all the boys had these? They kept throwing them at the walls to stick and the teachers got really angry."

Just then, Mia's mom and dad walked over with Alex on Mr. Greene's shoulders. "Hi, girls. Do you want some sparklers?" asked Mia's mom.

Mia's heart sank. Now there was no way she would get a chance to talk to the others. "It's okay, thanks. Aunt Carol just gave us some," she said.

"That's really kind of you, Carol," said Mia's mom.

"It's no problem at all, dear. Now I'd better go and help with the teas and coffees. Enjoy the fireworks, everyone!"

With a cheerful wave, Aunt Carol disappeared into the crowd.

"Carol's getting a lot more involved with town life than she used to," Mrs. Greene said to Mr. Greene.

"She must be lonely without Grandma Anne," he said. "They used to spend so much time together, didn't they?"

"Well, I'm glad she's keeping busy," said Mia's mom.

Alex suddenly spotted the stretchy man in Lexi's hands. "Me! Me!" he said, reaching out.

"No. They belong to the girls, Alex," said Mia's mom.

"Me want!" Alex's voice rose.

"It's okay. He can have mine," said Mia,

taking the stretchy man off her box of sparklers and giving it to her brother.

Just then, there was a shrill sound and a crackle as multicolored stars exploded into the dark sky.

"The fireworks are starting!" said Mia's mom.

Violet pulled Mia slightly away from the adults. "You were going to tell us something," she whispered.

The fireworks exploded overhead with a bang and a fountain of silver and gold stars. Mia shook her head. It was much too noisy to talk now, and there were people everywhere.

"I'll tell you tomorrow," she hissed. "Let's meet at the playground before school starts."

Violet nodded, and another firework erupted in the sky.

Mia woke early the next morning. To her relief, she hadn't had another nightmare about the Shades.

She glanced at her clock. There was still half an hour before she needed to get up for school. Bracken was snoozing beside her, his body stretched out along the comforter, his snout resting on her arm. She rubbed his head, and he wriggled up the bed and nuzzled her cheek with his cold nose. She giggled. "That tickles!"

Bracken rolled onto his back so she could scratch his tummy. "What are we doing today?" he asked.

"I've got school." Mia sighed. She glanced at her desk and saw the round pink stone there, glowing faintly in the dim light. She went over and picked it up.

"What do you have there?" Bracken asked.

"It's a Seeing Stone." Mia felt awkward.

"Aunt Carol gave it to me yesterday. She said I can use it to look into the past."

"But you don't need a Seeing Stone," said Bracken. "You can look into the past using the Star Magic."

"I didn't get a chance to tell her that I'd managed to do that," said Mia. "Maybe I should just try with this stone…. It might be easier." She gave him a hopeful look.

"Don't," Bracken said uneasily. "It doesn't feel right to me. You're a Star Friend. You should use Star Magic."

"Okay," Mia said. She sat down at her desk and dropped the stone into her lap. "I'll try this mirror again." She stared at the mirror on her desk and asked it to show her who put the gnome in Paige's yard.

But just like the day before, the image flickered and was too blurry to see clearly.

"It's no good." Mia glanced at her bedside clock. "Why don't I just try with the stone?

Aunt Carol thought it would help."

"All right," Bracken said, but he didn't sound happy about it.

Mia picked the stone out of her lap and gazed at it. "Show me the day the gnome arrived at Paige's house," she whispered. Excitement flared inside her as an image started to form inside it. Bracken paced around her chair, but Mia hardly noticed; she was much too busy staring at the image. Aunt Carol was right— she could do other types of magic! It felt different, though— as if her energy was being pulled into the pink stone.

She saw a woman in a raincoat with the hood pulled up, standing in the driveway of Paige's house by the trampoline. The person's back was to Mia, but then she half-turned. Mia gasped as she saw the Wish Gnome in her hands. She still couldn't see the woman's face clearly, but after she placed the gnome on the ground and stood up, the hood of the coat fell back, revealing short, iron-gray hair and a familiar face.

"Mrs. Crooks!" exclaimed Mia. She lowered the stone in shock. "Bracken! It was Mrs. Crooks!"

7
WHO IS MRS. CROOKS?

"I knew I didn't like that lady when I saw her in the woods," said Lexi as they huddled together in a far corner of the playground later that morning. Their breath was freezing in icy clouds on the air.

Mia nodded. "Mrs. Crooks hasn't been in town long, and the Shades only started appearing recently, too!"

"And there are two gnomes on her doorstep?" said Sita.

Mia nodded. "Yes, and she's the person who

gave the Wish Gnome to Paige's mom! I saw her with my magic."

"She has to be the one doing dark magic," said Violet.

Sita looked worried. "What if she puts Wish Shades into more gnomes and gives them to more people? Imagine all those people making wishes that are granted in a horrible way."

"We don't know for sure that Mrs. Crooks *is* the person who is conjuring Shades," Lexi pointed out. "We really need proof."

"I could try spying on her house through my mirror," Mia said. "I might see something that would prove she's using dark magic."

"Why don't you all ask if you can come to my house after school?" said Violet. "If Mia can't see anything, I could shadow-travel to Mrs. Crooks's house."

"That's too dangerous!" Sita protested.

"I can't meet tonight," said Lexi. "I have gymnastics."

"We shouldn't do anything without Lexi," said Sita quickly. "It's not fair."

Mia glanced at Lexi. She didn't want to leave her out, but if Violet was right about there being more Shades, they had to do something fast. "Do you want us to wait until tomorrow?" she asked Lexi.

"No," Lexi said reluctantly. "You should find out what's going on. Tomorrow I have piano, so I won't be able to meet up then, either. I'm not free after school until Wednesday. But promise you'll tell me everything!"

"Promise. I'll stop by your house tonight and fill you in," said Sita.

"Okay. Be careful!" Lexi told them.

Mia took a deep breath. "We will."

After school, the girls shut themselves in Violet's bedroom and called their animals. They sat on the floor, and Mia took out her pocket mirror. She felt the magic tingle through her.

Show me inside Mrs. Crooks's house, she thought.

An image appeared of a kitchen. There was a wooden table and two chairs, a dresser with some neatly stacked wildlife magazines, and a lot of brightly colored plastic bowls on the counter. Mia felt a flicker of disappointment. She wasn't quite sure what she had been expecting.

"I can see the kitchen," Mia told the others. "It just looks normal, though…." She broke off as the image in the mirror showed a door open. Mrs. Crooks came in, with the one-eared white dog at her heels.

"Time to go and check on the shed," she heard Mrs. Crooks saying. "They'll be ready to go soon."

Mia's eyes widened. *They'll be ready to go soon.* What was Mrs. Crooks talking about?

Mrs. Crooks bent down and rubbed the dog's head. "One day, they'll all be set free. That's what we want, isn't it?" The little dog ran to the back door and whined. Mrs. Crooks smiled. "All right. Let's go and see my beauties." She opened the back door, and they went out.

Mia slowly lowered the mirror.

"Well?" Violet demanded.

Mia's mouth felt dry. "Mrs. Crooks was talking to her dog about something she keeps in the shed. She said 'They'll be ready to go soon,' and something about setting them free."

Sita looked worried. "Do you think she has some Shades in her shed?"

"Can you look inside it?" Violet asked quickly.

"I'll try." Mia picked up the mirror again. *Inside Mrs. Crooks's shed*, she thought.

An image appeared. There was no light in the shed, and blinds were drawn across the windows, but Mia could just about make out some boxes. No. Not boxes. They were metal and wire-mesh cages. "There are cages in the shed!" Mia said to the others.

Sorrel hissed. "We need to investigate this more!"

Bracken leaped to his feet. "I agree! We need to look inside this shed."

"We might be able to spy on it from Aunt Carol's yard," said Mia. "Or even climb over the fence and get inside."

"Or shadow-travel inside," put in Violet.

"But what if there *are* Shades in there?" said Sita. "They might attack us. They've got such sharp nails, and they move so fast and—"

"Sita!" Mia put a hand on her arm. "Calm down."

Willow nuzzled Sita. "Don't be scared. We have to find out what's going on. It's what Star Friends do."

Sita took a trembling breath. "I know. I just hate Shades."

Mia squeezed her arm. "Don't worry. We'll all be together. Nothing bad will happen."

I hope, she added in her head.

8
SOMETHING STRANGE

Aunt Carol answered the door. "Hello, girls," she said in surprise.

"Can we please come in, Aunt Carol?" Mia said. "We need to use your yard."

Aunt Carol raised her eyebrows but ushered them inside. "So what's this about?" she asked as she shut the door.

"We think Mrs. Crooks might be the person conjuring the Shades," said Mia.

"No!" Aunt Carol gasped.

Mia nodded and told Aunt Carol about

the image of Mrs. Crooks with the gnome in Paige's yard. She explained what she had heard Mrs. Crooks saying and told her about the cages in the shed.

"I never liked that woman," said Aunt Carol, shaking her head.

"We need to try and find out exactly what's in her shed," said Violet. "Can we use your yard, please?"

"Of course. You can call your Star Animals, too, if you want," said Aunt Carol. "After all, it's not like you have to keep them a secret from me!"

"Thank you!" Mia said. She would feel much happier if they could have Bracken, Sorrel, and Willow with them.

They hurried through the house and out the back door to the yard. They whispered the names of their animals, and Bracken, Sorrel, and Willow appeared.

Mia heard Aunt Carol's intake of breath and

saw the elderly lady looking at the animals with
a strange expression.

Bracken shot Mia an uncertain look.

"Oh, don't you worry about me, dear,"
said Aunt Carol, backing into the house. "I'll
stay out of your way." She disappeared into
the house and then reappeared at the kitchen
window.

"Mia!" Bracken said anxiously. "You know
people shouldn't see us unless they're Star
Friends."

"It's only Aunt Carol, and she's seen Grandma Anne's Star Animal. Don't worry," said Mia.

"I smell Shades," said Sorrel, scenting the air. Her tail fluffed up. "All around here."

Willow went to the fence that separated Aunt Carol's yard from Mrs. Crooks's. "I can smell it here."

"The fence is too high for us to see over," Mia said. "If only Lexi was here, she'd be able to climb the fence."

"Lexi isn't the only one who can climb," said Sorrel. She jumped up and dug her claws into the side of the fence. In a few seconds, she was balancing on the top. "I can see the shed," she told them. "It's just on the other side. I'll try and see through the windows." She jumped down into Mrs. Crooks's yard.

Violet stepped toward a nearby patch of shadows.

"No!" Sita said, grabbing her. "Don't shadow-travel there, Violet. It could be dangerous. Let's wait and see what Sorrel finds out."

Violet looked like she was about to argue.

"Please stay," Sita repeated.

To Mia's surprise, Violet nodded. "Okay."

A few moments later, Sorrel reappeared at the top of the fence. "This yard definitely smells of Shades," she said, jumping down and wrinkling her nose in distaste.

"What did you find out?" Violet asked eagerly.

"Not a lot. I saw the cages through a gap in the shed wall, but I couldn't see into them. Oh, and there are gnomes in the yard."

"Gnomes," Mia echoed.

"Yes. Just like that one the Wish Shade was in. A bunch of them."

Mia shook her head. "This is weird."

"We need to get into that shed," said Violet.

"I'll shadow-travel into the yard and see if I can get inside."

Violet stepped toward the shadows, but as she did, Bracken's ears pricked up. "Wait! I hear the back door." He cocked his head to one side, listening. "Mrs. Crooks just came into the yard!"

Violet looked at Mia. "What do we do? I could use an illusion—disguise myself in some way and get into the yard. Or I could shadow-travel here tonight and look into the shed then."

"But you'd be on your own," Sita pointed out. "It's too risky." She took hold of Mia's and Violet's hands. "Look, I know you both want to do something right now, but remember how dangerous Shades are. And this time there might be a lot of them. Please don't do anything just yet. Let's talk to Lexi and Juniper first."

Mia wanted to argue, but maybe Sita was right. She found herself nodding and realized Violet was nodding, too.

"All right," Violet agreed.

"We'll wait," said Mia.

"Okay, good," said Sita, looking relieved. "I'll tell Lexi what we've found out. And then we can think of a plan."

Mia racked her brain, but by bedtime, she still hadn't thought of a way they could safely get into Mrs. Crooks's yard and see inside the shed. She tried spying on Mrs. Crooks, but all she saw was her making an omelette and watching a wildlife program on TV—nothing to suggest that Mrs. Crooks was doing dark magic.

As she snuggled in bed that night, she pulled Bracken close. "I hope I don't have any horrible dreams tonight."

He licked her cheek. "I'll wake you if you do."

She kissed his head and went to sleep with him curled up against her tummy.

She didn't have a nightmare, but her dreams

were full of strange images again—Sita staring at a patch of shadows in alarm, Lexi pacing anxiously around her bedroom, Violet sitting on her bed looking unhappy, a person in a hooded cloak, tiny figures scuttling through the shadows, and a night sky where the stars formed into words: *her power grows.*

When Mia woke up, she rubbed her eyes and yawned. She felt tired even though she had just had a whole night's sleep. She wondered what the images meant, especially the last one. Whose power was growing? Was it one of them or the person doing dark magic?

She gave Bracken a hug and then got up and went downstairs.

Her mom was in the kitchen with Alex on her lap.

"Morning," said Mia.

"Morning," said her mom, yawning.

"Are you all right?" Mia asked, thinking her mom looked just as tired as she felt.

"Alex kept having nightmares," said Mrs. Greene. "I think the fireworks upset him."

"Not fireworks. Beetle," said Alex solemnly. He cuddled closer to his mom. "Big beetle." He looked at Mia with wide eyes, and his lower lip trembled. "In my room!"

"It was just a bad dream, Alex," Mia said. "There are no beetles in your room."

Alex didn't look convinced. "Beetle," he said again.

"I know!" Mia hurried to the cupboard under the stairs where they kept all sorts of random things like gloves, umbrellas, and picnic blankets. She rummaged through one of the shelves and found what she was looking for. A plastic bug catcher! She'd liked to play with it when she was little, pressing the lever and clamping the plastic jaws around her toys. She took it back to Alex. "Here. If you see a beetle, you can pick it up with this and get rid of it." She picked a toy train off the floor to show him how it worked.

"Me do it!" Alex wriggled off his mom's lap and took the bug catcher from Mia, his nightmare forgotten.

"Thanks, Mia," her mom said with a smile.

Mia made herself some breakfast and then got ready for school. She desperately wanted to see the others. Maybe they had had some ideas. She sent them a text.

See u all at school before the bell! Mxx

A reply pinged back from Violet almost instantly.

Definitely! Can't wait to see u! xxxxxxx ☺☺☺

Mia blinked. Violet's texts were usually short, and she almost *never* used that many kisses and emojis. What was going on?

Her mom dropped her off early. The school playground was still almost empty. Violet was sitting on the wall at the edge of the playground. She came running over eagerly. "I thought you were never going to get here!"

Mia was surprised. "It's still early."

"I know, but I was worried." Violet's face took on an anxious expression that was very out of character. "You do still want to be friends with me, don't you?"

"Of course. Why?" Mia said in astonishment.

"Oh, nothing." Violet looked relieved. "It's just I had a dream last night that none of you wanted me to be a Star Friend. It felt so real." The anxious look crossed her face again. "It's not true, is it?"

"No," Mia reassured her. "Of course not. Everyone likes you. Although you might want to stop telling Lexi that you're better than she is at math," she added. "I think that annoys her

just a little bit."

Violet looked horrified. "Oh, no! I didn't mean to annoy her."

Mia was saved from replying by Sita arriving at the playground.

"Hi." Sita glanced over her shoulder as she reached them.

"Are you okay?" Mia said.

"Not really. I thought I saw something in the shadows when I was walking to school," whispered Sita. "It looked like a Shade!"

"A Shade!" echoed Mia and Violet.

"I thought I saw one last night, too," Sita told them. "It was in my room when I turned off my light. It was there for a minute, right by my closet, and then it disappeared."

Mia frowned. "What about Willow? Did she sense it?"

"I called her, and when she appeared, she said she could smell a Shade, but the scent was faint and it didn't seem to come from near the closet. The Shade had seemed so real and—"

She was interrupted by Violet suddenly waving madly. "Lexi, hi! Over here!" she called as Lexi came onto the playground. Lexi hurried over.

"Lexi! I never meant to upset you. I think you're great at math—really, really great!" Violet burst out.

Mia stared. It was like an over-friendly alien had invaded Violet's body! For a moment, she wondered if it could be a Shade…. But no, it wasn't making Violet horrible. It was making her super-nice.

Lexi looked surprised.

"You are so good at it," Violet carried on.

"No, I'm not," said Lexi gloomily. "I couldn't sleep last night. I kept thinking about that math challenge we did. I'm sure I've done badly on it. I think I failed my piano exam, too. What if I failed them both? I'm not looking forward to getting the results."

"You never fail anything," said Mia. "You'll be fine. Look, we need to think about Mrs. Crooks. Did Sita tell you everything last night?"

Lexi nodded.

"We need to get a good look inside that shed," said Mia. "Has anyone come up with any good ideas?"

"I bet you have," said Violet, smiling at her. "You're so great at thinking up ideas, Mia."

"Well, I haven't thought of anything yet," Mia

admitted. "Have you?"

Violet shook her head.

"Sita?" Mia asked.

"What?" Sita jumped as Mia said her name.

"Have you had any ideas?" Mia said.

"About what? About the Shade that's following me?"

"No," said Mia. "I really don't think there's a Shade following you. About Mrs. Crooks!"

"Oh … um … that," said Sita. "No, I haven't thought of anything."

"Me, neither," said Lexi. "The only things I can think about are my piano exam and the math challenge. I can't handle it if I've failed."

Mia felt like stamping her foot in frustration. What was up with her friends that morning? They were being really strange.

✦ ✦ ✦

By the time school had ended, Mia had come up with a plan. If she and Sita distracted Mrs.

Crooks at the front door, Violet could shadow-travel into the yard and try and see into the shed. However, her plans were dashed when Violet's mom told them that Violet had a dentist appointment after school.

"I'll have to miss it, Mom," said Violet. "We've got stuff planned."

"Oh, no," her mom said. "You can't miss the dentist."

Violet turned to Mia and Sita. "Don't do anything without me."

"We won't. We'll wait until tomorrow," Mia said. Even if they had wanted to, they needed Violet's shadow-traveling to make the plan work.

"Lexi will be able to meet up with us tomorrow, too," said Sita.

"So you promise you won't go off and do anything without me?" said Violet.

"I said we wouldn't!" Mia spoke slightly sharply.

"Now you're annoyed with me!" wailed Violet.

"I'm not!"

"You are."

"Come on, Violet," her mom insisted.

Violet reluctantly left, shooting backward glances at her friends.

"I have no idea what's up with her today," Mia said to Sita.

"She is being odd," agreed Sita. "I'm glad we're not going to Mrs. Crooks's house, though. What if there are Shades in the shed?"

"Then we have to deal with them," said Mia firmly. "If Mrs. Crooks is doing dark magic, we have to stop her, Sita. You know we do."

Sita swallowed. "Y-yes. I guess."

Mia sighed. "I'll see you tomorrow."

"You're not going over to anyone's house today?" Mia's mom asked in surprise as Mia joined her. "That's unusual. How about we stop and see Aunt Carol then?"

"Okay," said Mia. "Where's Alex?" she asked.

"At home with Dad. He had such a bad night's sleep that he didn't go to his playgroup today. So how was school?"

"Okay," said Mia, thinking about how strangely her friends had been behaving. She couldn't wait to get home and talk to Bracken about it. Could it be because of some sort of dark magic?

When they reached the row of houses where Aunt Carol lived, Mia saw Mrs. Crooks's dog watching through her front window. He barked when he saw her, and Mrs. Crooks appeared. Seeing Mia, she scowled and closed the curtains. "Come on, Mia," her mom called as Aunt Carol answered her front door.

"How lovely to see you both. I have some friends here," said Aunt Carol. "We're planning the Christmas fair."

"Oh, we won't bother you, then," Mrs. Greene said.

"No, no, come in and have a cup of tea with us. Please."

Mia's heart sank. The ladies all greeted her and her mom warmly.

"I'll just put the kettle on. Mia, would you like a hot chocolate?" Aunt Carol said.

"Yes, please," said Mia.

"Why don't you come and give me a hand?" said Aunt Carol.

Leaving her mom to chat, Mia went into the kitchen with her. "So," Aunt Carol lowered her voice to a whisper and beckoned Mia closer. "Have you found out anything else about you-know-who?" She gestured toward Mrs. Crooks's house.

"No," Mia whispered back. "Not yet."

"I've been watching her. She went out late last night with a basket. I think she might be collecting herbs and plants to do magic with.

Shades can be conjured using potions. Did
you know that?"

Mia's heart beat faster. "No."

"We need to keep an eye on her," said Aunt
Carol. "She could have a secret place she goes
to when she wants to work magic."

"In the woods, maybe?" Mia said.

"It's very likely," Aunt Carol agreed,
nodding. "I'll try and watch her using my
crystals. Have you tried doing magic with the
Seeing Stone
I gave you?"

"Yes, and it worked!" Mia said. "I saw into
the past. That was how I saw Mrs. Crooks
with the gnome at Paige's."

Aunt Carol smiled. "Great job. You're
obviously very talented at magic."

Mia glowed. "Do you really think so?"

"Yes, I do," Aunt Carol said. She gave her a
curious look. "Why do you ask?"

"Well, it's just that one of the Shades we

fought said that one of us would be really powerful—more powerful than the person doing dark magic."

Aunt Carol leaned closer. "Did the Shade say which of you it would be?"

"I don't know. He didn't—" Mia broke off as her mom came in.

Mrs. Greene laughed as they both jumped. "What are you two whispering about?"

Aunt Carol chuckled. "Oh, it's just a silly little secret we have," she said, tapping her nose and looking at Mia. "Isn't that right, Mia?"

Mia nodded.

Aunt Carol smiled brightly at Mrs. Greene. "Let's have some tea!"

9
DARK MAGIC AT WORK!

Mia was anxious to tell the others what Aunt Carol had said about people being able to conjure Shades using potions, but when she got to school the next day, they were all still acting oddly. She found Lexi sitting on a bench, her head buried in her spelling book. "We've got a test today. I'm sure I'm going to fail," she muttered. "I can't talk now."

"Lexi, you're awesome at spelling. You won't fail. I need to talk to you, though. This is important!" Mia said.

"Not as important as my test." Lexi got up. "You don't get it!" She ran off.

Before Mia could go after her, Sita arrived. Her eyes were wide and scared.

"Mia! I'm sure there's a Shade following me!" she hissed as she raced up to her. "It was in our yard this morning and then behind some trees on the way to school. One minute it's there, the next it's gone."

"Let's go to the wall and talk there," said Mia.

"Okay, and there's something else I need to talk to you about, too," said Sita. "I'm sure it's not true, but Willow said I should mention it to you all."

As they walked over to the wall, Violet came running up.

"Where are you two going? Why weren't you waiting for me? You don't like me, do you? I knew it!" Her eyes filled with tears as she looked from Mia to Sita.

"Don't be silly!" Mia said in astonishment.

"Violet, I saw a Shade," said Sita.

"Where?" said Violet.

"In the trees, in the yard…."

Mia sighed. "Sita thinks he's following her, but…."

Violet glared. "So you've been talking about it without me? Leaving me out?"

"No!" Mia protested.

"I knew you didn't want to be friends with me!" Violet said, and fighting back a sob, she hurried away.

"Okay," Mia said in despair. "Why are you all behaving so strangely?"

"Look, in the shadows over there!" gasped Sita, pointing to a nearby hedge. Mia looked, but there was nothing there. She let magic flow into her and used her powers to see if there was anything she couldn't detect with her normal vision. Nothing.

"Sita, there really isn't a Shade there," she said. "I'm sure of it."

The bell rang, and Sita breathed a sigh of relief. "I'm going inside. It won't follow me there!"

Mia was beginning to think that somehow a Shade was affecting her friends. But what was it trying to do? Was there a type of Shade that just made people behave oddly? And if it was affecting her friends, why wasn't it affecting her?

Oh, Bracken, I wish I could talk to you right now! she thought.

After school, no one wanted to meet up. Lexi wanted to go home in case the mail carrier had delivered her exam results, Violet was still refusing to talk to Mia and Sita, and Sita said she wanted to stay with her mom.

As soon as Mia got home, she called Bracken.

"What is it?" he asked her. "You look upset."

Mia hugged him and told him in a rush what they had been doing.

"Why don't I go and talk to Willow, Sorrel, and Juniper?" Bracken said. "If a Shade has been anywhere near the others, Sorrel and Willow will definitely have smelled it."

"Can you just go off and talk to them?" said Mia. A thought struck her.

"I can call them using Star Magic, and we can meet each other if we go to the clearing," Bracken replied. "The clearing is special because Star Magic is strong there. The waterfall is a link between this world and the

Star World. I'll be back as soon as I can."

Mia kissed his head, and he disappeared.

Once he left, the minutes seem to drag by. She picked up her mirror. Maybe while she was waiting, she should use her magic…. But what would she ask to see?

Sita, she decided.

A picture of her friend appeared in the mirror. She was with Willow in her bedroom.

"I still haven't talked to the others about it, Willow," she was saying.

"You must," Willow said softly.

"But what do you think they'll say?" A noise made Sita jump. "The Shade! I just saw it again!"

"Sita, there's nothing there," said Willow.

Mia shook her head and tried Violet next.

Violet was sitting on her bed, her arms pulled tight around her knees. Sorrel was nudging her head against Violet's arm.

"No one likes me, Sorrel," Violet was saying.

"Mia and Sita keep going off and leaving me out."

We don't, Mia thought. *What's she talking about?*

"They don't want to be friends, and Lexi has never liked me," Violet went on. "I'm never going to have any real friends, am I?" She sounded so despairing. Her usual air of confidence had completely vanished.

"I'm your friend. I'll always be here for you," Sorrel said, her voice soft for once. "Please don't be upset, Violet. This isn't like you." She nuzzled Violet's cheek. Suddenly she stiffened, her head tilting to one side. "Violet, Bracken is calling me. I need to go. He wouldn't be calling me unless it was important."

Mia let the image fade and tried Lexi. She was pacing around her bedroom. "I'm going to fail, I'm going to fail," she was whispering. "Oh, what am I going to do?"

Juniper wasn't there. Mia wondered if he was

with Bracken and the others in the woods.

Mia put down the mirror. Her friends all seemed so unhappy. She ran her hands through her hair. She didn't know what to do about her friends, and she didn't know what to do about Mrs. Crooks. Were the two things connected?

Mia felt like she had pieces of a jigsaw puzzle laid out in front of her, but she just couldn't seem to put the picture together.

A few minutes later, there was a shimmer of light, and Bracken reappeared.

"I've spoken to the other animals, Mia."

"And?" Mia demanded.

"They all agree something strange is going on. Sorrel and Willow have both smelled the faint scent of dark magic in Violet and Sita's bedrooms, although they say the smell comes and goes. They're worried."

"What do we do, Bracken?" Mia said. "Should we try and find out what's going on with them, or should we try and find out more about Mrs. Crooks? If only the others weren't so distracted."

Bracken yipped and pricked his ears. "Mia! Maybe that's it! If Mrs. Crooks has somehow found out you're all Star Friends, she might be using magic to distract them."

Mia frowned. "But why just Lexi, Sita, and Violet? Surely she'd want to distract me, too."

Bracken's ears lowered. "Yes, you're right. That doesn't make sense," he admitted.

"Mia!" Cleo called from outside the room. "Mom says dinner is ready."

"Coming!" Mia got to her feet. "I'll be back as soon as I can," she promised Bracken.

Mia's mom had cooked lasagna for dinner, Mia's favorite, but she was so worried about what was going on that she didn't feel like

eating. Alex didn't seem to want his, either. He pushed it around his plate and kept throwing his fork on the floor.

"Come on, Alex, eat up," said Cleo, picking up a spoonful of lasagna from his plate. "Here comes the train. Choo-choo!"

"No!" Alex wailed, swinging his hand and sending the spoon flying.

Mrs. Greene rubbed her forehead wearily. "Don't worry, Cleo. He's just really tired." Standing up, she lifted Alex out of his chair. "Let's go and get you into your pajamas, Alex-boy."

"I'll take him upstairs, Mom," offered Mia. Her mom looked really tired.

"Thanks, sweetie." Mrs. Greene smiled. "Once he has his pjs on, he can come down and have some milk, and I'll read him a story."

Mia nodded and swung Alex onto her hip. "Up we go," she said, heading for the door.

Alex clutched her as they reached the stairs.

"Beetle! No!"

"What do you mean, beetle?" she said.

He struggled. "In my room. Beetle!"

"There aren't beetles in your room, Alex. You just saw them in a nightmare."

"No." He shook his head. "Big beetle!"

They reached the top of the stairs. Mia put him down. "All right, if there's a big beetle, I'll get rid of it," she said. "Let me take a look." She pushed open the bedroom door. Alex's room looked just like it usually did. "See, no beetles."

Alex came slowly into the room. He stiffened and pointed at the closet.

"Beetle!" he whispered, his eyes growing wide as saucers.

"Don't be silly, there isn't a—" Mia broke off with a squeak as a large black beetle leg appeared out of one of the closet doors.

"Mai-Mai!" cried Alex, grabbing her around the knees.

Mia stared. What was going on? Suddenly, the closet doors flew open, revealing an enormous beetle with red eyes and sharp pincers. Rearing up on its back legs, it leaped out of the closet!

10
DISCOVERING THE SHADE

Mia hardly paused to think—she opened
herself to the magic current. When she was
using her magic, she could see where things
were going to move a second or two before
they did it. But the magic allowed her to
see something else, too. There was a glowing
outline around the beetle. It wasn't a real beetle.
It was just an illusion!

"I don't believe in you!" she said, pointing at
it. "You're not real."

The beetle paused.

"You are *not* real!" she repeated firmly.

The beetle vanished in a flash of light.

"Gone!" said Alex in surprise. "Beetle go poof!"

Mia breathed a sigh of relief. "Yes, beetle go poof!" she said. Crouching down, she pulled Alex to her and hugged him. "If it comes back, you just have to tell it you don't believe in it. You mustn't be scared—it's not real." She couldn't help wondering why on earth there was a beetle illusion in her little brother's room.

As she pulled Alex close, something fell out of his pants pocket. It was the stretchy man Mia

had given him at the fireworks display. Picking it up, she put it on his bookcase next to the bug catcher. "Come on, now, let's put your pajamas on."

She helped him get changed and took him back downstairs to their mom, then ran to her room and quickly told Bracken everything that had happened.

"I just don't understand," she said. "Why was there a beetle illusion in Alex's room?"

"It could be a Fear Shade," said Bracken. "They discover people's fears and use illusions to make it seem like those fears are coming to life. The more scared the person gets, the stronger the illusion grows."

"Do you think Fear Shades could be affecting Lexi, Sita, and Violet, too?" Mia said slowly. "Lexi's been really scared about her exam results, Sita's been terrified there's a Shade following her, and Violet…." She paused. "Well, Violet's been convinced we don't like her, but I'm not sure what that has to do with being scared."

"Unless she's scared about not having any friends," said Bracken.

Mia let out a breath. "Of course!" Violet might often act as if she didn't need anyone at all, but she'd been really happy since they'd become friends. Her fear *was* being without friends again. Suddenly, she remembered something. "Bracken! In my nightmare the other night, the Shades said, 'We will make your fears come true!' Well, people's fears *are* coming true—or at least it seems as if they are."

Bracken spun in a circle. "We need to find the objects the Shades are trapped in. What do all your friends have?"

"It has to be something Alex has, too." Mia shook her head. "I can't think of anything like that…." Then she gasped. "Oh, yes, I can! It's the little yellow stretchy men, Bracken! They were attached to the sparkler boxes that Aunt

Carol gave us on bonfire night. I gave my little man to Alex, and the others all kept theirs. But hang on—" she paused, frowning—"Aunt Carol wouldn't give us something with dark magic in it. Unless…." She started to nod as she made sense of it. "Unless she didn't know. She said she didn't remember the little men being attached to the sparkler boxes when she bought them at the store. Someone must have stuck them on afterward! It could have been Mrs. Crooks, even. After all, she lives next door!"

"We have to get a hold of those stretchy men," said Bracken.

"There's one in Alex's bedroom," said Mia. "Come on, no one's around."

They ran along the landing and into Alex's room, and Mia shut the door. Her eyes fell on the little yellow stretchy man sitting on the bookcase where she had left it.

No. She frowned. She'd left it on the top shelf, and now it was on the second shelf down.

Her skin prickled.

"Come here, you!" she whispered, reaching out.

The stretchy man jumped away from her. It scuttled along the shelf and then turned to face her. Its round face became pointed, its hands grew claw-like nails, and its face twisted into an evil smile.

With a growl, Bracken leaped at it, but it jumped down to the floor. Mia grabbed hold of it, but it bit her hard with its sharp teeth. "Ow!" she gasped, dropping it. It raced toward the door, but Bracken was there in a flash. He leaped in front of it and crouched down, blocking the way. "You're not getting out."

"Oh, I think I am," the stretchy man hissed. "I'll find someone else whose fears I can make come true." He stretched his hands, and his nails grew even longer. "Move, fox, or you'll be sorry!"

"Not as sorry as you'll be for scaring my brother!" Mia grabbed the plastic bug catcher she'd given Alex and clamped the jaws shut over the stretchy man, trapping him inside. "Gotcha!" she said, holding him up.

"No!" the stretchy man screeched, hammering his little fists against the plastic container.

"Oh, yes, and now you and all the other Shades are going back to the shadows where you belong!" Mia picked up a metal tin that Alex kept cars in. She emptied it and dropped the stretchy man inside, releasing the jaws of the bug catcher and slamming down the lid.

Bracken spun in a circle. "Yay, Mia! You got him!"

Mia grinned. "One down, three to go!"

11
SITA'S SURPRISE

Mia persuaded her dad to drive her to Violet's house by telling him that they had some homework they needed to do together. She thought it would be best to go to Violet's first, then she and Violet could shadow-travel to Lexi and Sita's houses together. Violet's mom, Mrs. Cooper, answered the door.

"Hello," she said, looking a little puzzled. "Violet didn't mention you were coming over this evening."

"She didn't?" Mia said innocently. "We

arranged it at school."

"Well, come on in. She's in her room."

Mia hurried up the stairs and knocked on Violet's bedroom door.

"What is it?" Violet sounded upset.

"Violet, it's me—Mia."

"Mia?" The door opened. Violet's cheeks were tear-stained. "What are you doing here?"

Mia shut the door behind her. "Bracken!" she whispered. He appeared in a shimmer. "Call Sorrel," Mia urged Violet.

Violet looked confused but did what Mia said. "Sorrel!"

"What's happening?" said the wildcat as soon as she appeared. Her back arched, and she glared at Mia's bag. "Your bag smells like dark magic!"

"I'll tell you more about that in a moment," said Mia. "But first, Violet—"

"Why are you here?" interrupted Violet. "You don't like me. You, Sita, and Lexi don't

want to be friends with me. I bet you all talk
about me behind my back. None of you wants
me to be a Star Friend." Her eyes brimmed
with hurt. "You wish I'd never been chosen."

Mia wondered what to do. She'd been able
to make the beetle vanish simply by saying she
didn't believe in it, but Violet's fears were all in
her head.

"Sorrel is the only friend I've got," said
Violet miserably.

"That's not true!" Mia said. "Violet, I'm your
friend. Please believe me."

Violet looked at her tearfully.

"It's true," said Bracken, licking her hand. "After you fought the last Shade, Mia told me how glad she was that you were a Star Friend and how happy she was that you were friends again."

"I think it's a Shade that's making you feel differently," said Mia.

"A Shade?" Violet echoed.

"Impossible," said Sorrel. "I would know if a Shade had been affecting Violet."

"You said you'd smelled the traces of a Shade here. Well, it's been moving around," said Bracken. "Probably so that you wouldn't catch it."

"Where is it?" said Sorrel, looking around. "What's it trapped in?"

"Violet, you know that little yellow stretchy man you got on bonfire night?" Mia said. "The Shade is inside it. There's one in my bag at the moment. We caught it at my house and put it in a tin. It made Alex think there was a giant beetle in his room."

"They're Fear Shades, I think," Bracken said. "Shades that make people believe their worst fears are coming true."

"Alex is scared of beetles, so he saw a giant beetle," said Mia. "Lexi's biggest fear is failing exams, and I think the Shade in her house is making her believe that's going to happen—"

"Sita's really scared of Shades, so her Shade has made her believe that there's one following her," Violet broke in. "And me … it's been making me think that no one likes me."

"You don't need to be scared of that!" Mia burst out. "We all like you. I mean, I know sometimes you and Lexi don't get along, but we all want you to be our friend. We're all glad you're a Star Friend—Lexi, too." She grabbed Violet's hands. "I promise I'm telling the truth."

As their eyes met, Violet swallowed. "I

believe you," she said slowly. Her expression gradually cleared. "I've been so silly!" she exclaimed, pulling away from Mia. "But the feelings I had seemed so real...."

Mia nodded. "The Shade made you believe them."

"Where is this Shade?" hissed Sorrel, her tail fluffing out.

There was a sinister chuckle, and a small, yellow stretchy man looked out from behind the mirror on Violet's desk.

"Looks like I've been discovered," he said. "And I was having such fun making Violet think everyone hated her. Tricked you!" He gave a squeaky laugh.

Sorrel sprang onto the desk. The stretchy man somersaulted off and lightly landed on the floor.

"Can't catch me!" he chortled.

He shot across the floor, heading for the slightly open window.

Bracken was after him in a flash, jaws
snapping, but the stretchy man zoomed up the
wall, using his sticky hands and feet. He
reached for the window ledge
and then recoiled with a
high-pitched gasp as sharp
spikes suddenly shot out
of the windowsill.

"What?" he cried.

Losing his grip, he tumbled
through the air, his limbs
waving. As he landed on the floor,
Sorrel sprang from the table and caught
him in her jaws.

"Let me go!" squawked the stretchy man.

Mia pulled the tin out of her bag and
opened the lid, and Sorrel spat the man inside.
Mia banged the lid back on.

"What just happened?" the little man
screeched.

"I think you'll find *I* just tricked *you*!" said

Violet. "You're not the only one who can cast illusions! I made you see what wasn't there!"

"No!" the little man shrieked, banging at the tin.

"Two down, two to go," said Mia, high-fiving Violet.

Sorrel gave a smug meow, and Bracken bounded over. "Now, that's what I call teamwork!" he said.

"Ugh!" Sita squealed as Violet and Mia suddenly appeared in the shadows by her closet. She and Willow leaped to the far side of her bedroom and stared at them with wide eyes.

"Violet? Mia? Is it really you?" Sita cried.

"Yes, we shadow-traveled here together," said Mia, going over to her. She looked at Bracken. "Bracken, guard the door. We'll have to vanish if anyone comes."

"I thought it was the Shade who's been following me!" Sita said. "I—" She broke off with a gasp and pointed to the closet. "The Shade! Look! There it is!"

Hearing a low, sinister laugh, they swung around. A tall figure stepped out of the shadows. Its limbs were angular, its fingers tipped with spiky nails. "Sita, oh, Sita," it hissed.

For a moment, Mia felt her blood freeze. But then she came to her senses. "You're not real!" she said, marching over to it. "I don't believe in you!" And with that, the Shade vanished in a cloud of smoke.

Sita gaped. "What … what's going on?"

"The Shade was an illusion, Sita. There hasn't really been a Shade following you," said Violet. "But there has been one affecting you."

"Where's the yellow stretchy man you got at the bonfire? The Shade is trapped inside that," said Mia.

"It's in my coat pocket downstairs," said Sita.

"Go and get it," urged Violet.

Sita hurried out of the room and returned a few moments later with her coat. She pulled the little stretchy man out of the pocket. "There's a Shade inside this?"

"Yes, one who's been making you imagine that a Shade is following you," said Mia.

As they spoke, the little man started to laugh. Violet snatched him from Sita before she could drop him. "The tin, Mia! Ow!" she yelped. The stretchy man had grown fangs, and it bit Violet's fingers, but she didn't let go.

Mia pulled out the tin, and they stuffed the stretchy man inside with the other two.

"Horrible creature!" said Violet, shaking her

injured hand.

"Here, I can heal you," said Sita.

She touched Violet's hand and breathed in deeply. Before their eyes, the wound closed up. Violet smiled at Sita.

"So, there wasn't really a Shade following me? It was just an illusion?" Sita said.

"Yes, caused by that Shade," said Mia. "I think that Mrs. Crooks has somehow figured out that we're Star Friends, and she stuck those stretchy men to the sparklers before Aunt Carol gave them to us."

"But why?" said Sita.

"To distract us from following her!"

Sita frowned. "But she'd only just met us earlier that day."

"Well," said Mia, realizing that Sita was right, "maybe she knew we were Star Friends before she actually met us. That could be why she was so horrible to us in the clearing."

"Okay, but if she was putting Shades into

the stretchy men, why does she have all those gnomes?" Sita said.

Mia frowned. She couldn't think of an answer to that.

"Right now, we don't have time to figure this out," said Violet. "We have to help Lexi." She held out her hands. "Come on, let's shadow-travel!"

When they arrived in Lexi's room, everything was neat and tidy, like always, but Lexi was sitting on the floor with a letter in her hands, in tears. Juniper was smoothing her hair with his little paws. "Don't cry, please don't cry," he was begging.

"But I failed my piano exam." Lexi picked up another letter from the floor beside her. "And the math challenge."

"Hi, Lexi!" Mia said.

Lexi almost jumped out of her skin.

The girls called their animals' names, and they appeared, too.

Lexi stared. "Why are you all here? What's going on?" she whispered.

"Well, it's like this—" Violet began.

"Shh!" Lexi said hastily. "Mom and Dad are downstairs!"

"We'll be quiet," promised Mia in a quiet voice.

"Well, we'll try," said Sita, looking around anxiously.

"So why did you come?" demanded Lexi. "Was it because you heard about my exam results?" She held up the letters. "I failed math and piano."

"I don't think you did." Mia really hoped she was right. She let magic tingle through her. To her relief, the letters in Lexi's hand started to glow with a shining outline. "They're just an illusion!" She touched them. "You're not real," she said.

When the letters vanished, Lexi gasped.
"What happened?"

"A Fear Shade made those letters appear,"
Mia explained. "It made you believe your fears
were coming true. You haven't failed your
exams."

Lexi stared. "Really? Oh my goodness, I've
been so worried. So it was all a Shade?"

The others nodded.

There was a slight rustling noise, and
Bracken and Sorrel swung around to see a
stretchy man creeping across Lexi's desk.

"There it is!" said Bracken.

The stretchy man started to run, but in a flash, Juniper had jumped onto the table and grabbed him in his paws. "You're going nowhere!" Juniper exclaimed.

"Except for back to the shadows!" added Violet.

The stretchy man struggled in Juniper's grasp.

Mia took the tin out of her bag and opened it just enough to get the little man in and then slammed it shut. "Got him!" She looked at the others. "Now what do we do?"

"We need to send them back to the shadows," said Lexi.

"How exactly do you plan to do that?" said Sorrel. "Do I have to remind you that Violet must be looking a Shade in the eyes to be able to command it? That may be a problem."

Mia bit her lip. Sorrel was right. The stretchy men moved so fast when they were free—and there were four of them. How could Violet hope to be able to look them all in the eye at the same time?

"Maybe we should try sending them back one at a time," said Lexi. "If we open the tin and take one out, Violet could try and command it."

The lid on the tin shifted upward slightly as the stretchy men inside tried to get out.

"We'd better be quick!" said Sita. "This could go horribly wrong if they all escape."

"Okay, let's open the lid," said Lexi. "Violet, get ready."

"Remember, they bite," warned Mia. "Here goes!" She loosened one corner of the lid of the tin.

WHAM! The lid exploded off the tin, and the stretchy men leaped out.

Sita screamed, and Mia ducked as one jumped over her shoulder. Violet staggered back as another launched itself straight at her face with its claws out. Luckily Lexi saw what

was happening and, using her super-speed, she sprang in front of Violet and batted it away just in time. It flew through the air and landed on the floor.

"Thank you!" Violet gasped.

The animals sprang into action, trying to pounce and grab, but the stretchy men seemed to be everywhere. One of them reached the door, and Mia realized the man was planning on squeezing underneath it.

"Stop it!" she cried.

Mia and Violet both threw themselves forward, but even as Mia felt her fingers close around it, it seemed to slip out from between her fingers.

"It's escaping!" cried Violet.

"Freeze! Everyone, freeze!" exclaimed Sita.

All of a sudden, Mia found that she couldn't move. What was going on? She could see that everyone—her friends, the animals, and even the stretchy men—were frozen in their tracks.

"Oh," Sita said faintly, looking around the room. "I didn't think it would work that well."

Mia's thoughts raced. How had Sita made everyone do as she said?

Sita took a trembling breath. "Okay, listen to me. Mia, Lexi, and Violet, I want you all to unfreeze. Bracken, Willow, Juniper, and Sorrel, too. *Unfreeze!*"

It was as if a magic wand had been waved. Suddenly, Mia found she could move again.

"What's going on?" Lexi said, staring at Sita, who was standing in the middle of the room looking sheepish.

Willow trotted over to Sita. "Your magic, Sita," she said softly. "It's just as we thought."

"I know," said Sita in a small voice. "I'm not sure I like it." Willow nuzzled her.

"What are you talking about?" demanded Violet.

"Yes, enough of talking in riddles. Will one of you please explain what just happened?" said Sorrel sharply.

Sita put her hand on Willow's head. "Um … we were planning to tell you all about it, but then everything started going wrong, and I couldn't focus on anything other than the Shade I thought was following me. You know we all thought my magic had to do with healing and soothing people?"

They all nodded.

"Well, it *is* about healing, but I think that the soothing part isn't quite what it seems. People do calm down when I tell them to…." She glanced at Willow for help.

"But it's because Sita's magic lets her command others," explained Willow. "If she tells them to do something, they have to do it. People, animals, Shades."

Mia looked around at the four little stretchy men still frozen in position—one halfway under the door, one crouching down, one bending over, one on his tummy. Their eyes were rolling furiously as they fought against the magic, but they couldn't move.

"That's awesome," breathed Lexi.

"And scary," said Sita, with a slight shake to her voice.

"Sita, you must be the really powerful one the Shade told us about!" Mia realized.

"But I don't want to be," Sita said.

"I don't think you have a choice," said Bracken.

Sorrel gazed at Sita. "You will be in danger. A person using dark magic would do anything for your kind of power."

"Oh," Sita whispered.

Lexi picked up a frozen stretchy man that was lying near to her. "Look, let's talk about this more after we've sent these Shades back to the shadows." She looked at Willow. "Can Sita do that?"

"No, Sita can command them in this world, but only a Spirit Speaker like Violet can send spirits between worlds," Willow said.

"But what Sita can do is command the Shades to look Violet in the eyes," said Sorrel.

She picked up a stretchy man in her mouth and held it up to Violet.

Lexi nudged Sita. "Go on then. Do your commanding thing."

"Stretchy men, I … um … want you all to look at Violet," said Sita.

Sure enough, all four stretchy men reluctantly looked at Violet.

"Go back to the shadows where you

belong!" Violet said. The Shades shivered and shook and then, with a last wide-eyed look, they fell still.

"It worked!" said Sita in delight.

The animals bounded around the room.

"Great job, Sita," said Willow.

"That was amazing!" yapped Bracken.

"Shh!" said Lexi, glancing toward the door.

"You did exceptionally well," Sorrel purred to Violet.

"The Shades are really gone," Violet said in a low voice. "It's over!"

Mia shook her head. "No, it's not."

"What do you mean?" said Violet.

Mia took a deep breath. "We've still got Mrs. Crooks to deal with."

12
THE REAL MRS. CROOKS

Violet grabbed Mia's hand. "Time to shadow-travel to Mrs. Crooks's house!"

"No," said Sita quickly. "Not now. It's late. Imagine what will happen if our parents come looking for us and we're not in our bedrooms! They might even have discovered we're missing already."

Mia hesitated, but Sita was right. "Okay, we'll go over to her house tomorrow after school then."

The others all nodded.

They said good-bye to Lexi and all their
Star Animals, and then Violet shadow-
traveled with Sita and Mia back to Sita's
house. Leaving Sita there, they went on
to Violet's. As they arrived in the shadows
beside her closet, there was a knock on her
bedroom door.

"Do you two need anything?" Violet's mom
said, opening the door and looking in. "How's
the homework going?"

"Fine. We just finished, Mom," said Violet,
smoothing down her hair.

Mia nodded. "I'll call my dad and ask him to
come and get me."

"Don't worry. I can bring you home,"
Violet's mom said.

Mia and Violet shared a look of relief—that
had been close. What would have happened if
they hadn't gotten back in time? Shadow-travel
was amazing but very risky.

As Mrs. Cooper drove Mia and Violet past

Mrs. Crooks's house on the way back to her house, Mia wondered what Mrs. Crooks was doing. All the lights were off in the house. Was she out in the woods gathering plants and herbs to do more dark magic? Mia shivered. How could they possibly stop her?

Sita, Mia realized, thinking of Sita's new power. She'd be able to command Mrs. Crooks. *Tomorrow,* Mia thought. *Tomorrow we'll stop the dark magic once and for all.*

After school the next day, the girls asked if they could go for a walk and then have dinner at Mia's house. To their relief, all their parents agreed. They headed to Mrs. Crooks's house and stopped on the street. "Okay," said Violet. "As soon as she opens the door, you've got to use your magic, Sita, and make her ask us in. Then, once we're in, you need to command her to tell us about the dark magic she's been doing."

"I'm scared," said Sita, her eyes wide.

Mia squeezed her hand. "Don't be. We'll all be with you."

They started to walk down the driveway, but before they could reach the door, Mrs. Crooks came out. "What are you girls doing here?" she demanded.

Her dog ran out and started barking at them. It snapped at Sita's ankles, making her squeal and back away.

"Jack! Stop that! Come here!" called Mrs. Crooks. "You girls, go away!" she said angrily. "You heard me! Go away! Stop upsetting my dog!"

With all the noise and confusion, Sita didn't have a chance to try and use her magic on Mrs. Crooks.

"We're not upsetting him!" Violet shouted.

"What's going on here?" Hearing a familiar voice, Mia swung around and saw Mary from the Copper Kettle bakery. "Jenny, what's happening?

Jack, come here! Stop making all that noise."

To Mia's surprise, the dog stopped barking and ran over to Mary, greeting her with a wagging tail. Mary took hold of his collar.

"These children are bothering him, Mary," said Mrs. Crooks angrily. "Hanging around on my driveway. Trying to upset him."

Mary shook her head. "These girls are sweet. They wouldn't do that—they all adore animals."

Mrs. Crooks harrumphed.

"Girls, I'm sorry about this. Please excuse my sister," Mary said to them. "She's not very fond of young people."

Mia stared. Mary and horrible Mrs. Crooks were sisters? Yes, now that she looked, she could see similarities between them, but Mary's face was open and smiling, whereas Mrs. Crooks's was closed and suspicious.

"Calm down, Jenny. I promise you, these girls wouldn't ever hurt an animal. Would you, girls?" Mary went on.

"Never! We all love animals," said Violet.

"We really do," Lexi said, holding her hand out to the dog. He growled.

"I'm sorry, Lexi," Mary said. "Jack's not very good with young people. He was a stray who was badly treated by some teenagers once. That's why he only has one ear. He came into the vet's where Jenny used to work. She helped get him better and then adopted him."

"Oh," Mia said slowly.

"Jenny's working at the new wildlife sanctuary," Mary went on.

Mia's mind spun as she tried to match Mrs. Crooks the conjurer of Shades with Mrs. Crooks the animal lover whom Mary was telling her about.

"We have badgers and foxes and rabbits," said Mrs. Crooks, slightly gruffly. "And squirrels and weasels. Some of the animals we keep away from visitors—those who aren't too badly injured and who are going to be released back into the wild. The ones that need a lot of care become too trusting of people, so they have to stay at the sanctuary. They're often injured because of young people—" she gave them a stern look—"leaving litter in the woods. But Mary's right. If you like wildlife, you should come and visit."

Mary smiled. "Maybe today they could take a quick look in your shed, Jenny."

Shed! Mia saw the others' eyes all widen.

Mrs. Crooks nodded. "I don't see why not. Provided you're quiet and don't touch anything,"

"What's in the shed?" Violet ventured.

A rare smile lifted the corners of Mrs. Crooks's mouth. "Animals," she said. "Would you like to see?"

The girls exchanged looks. For a moment, Mia wondered if Mary and Mrs. Crooks were doing dark magic together. She wanted to see inside the shed—after all, it was what they had come here for—but was it an elaborate trap?

"Um … our parents probably wouldn't like us to come in without getting permission first," Lexi said slowly.

"Of course," said Mary. "Good girls. That's very sensible of you."

Just then a car pulled up. "Hi, girls," said Mia's mom, putting down the window. "Is everything okay?"

"Everything's fine," said Mary.

"Mom—" Mia felt a little nervous, but she knew she had to get to the bottom of this— "Mrs. Crooks just asked us if we want to see inside her shed. Is it okay if we do?"

"Jenny has some animals in there," said Mary.

"Sure," said Mrs. Greene. "I'm just popping over to the store to get some cheese and pepperoni. I can pick you up on the way back. Dad made some pizza dough, so you can make your own pizzas for dinner."

The girls nodded and followed Mrs. Crooks into the house. There were pictures of animals on the walls, and the kitchen smelled of baking bread.

"Come this way," said Mrs. Crooks.

As the girls stepped through the back door into the yard, they all gasped. There were pottery gnomes everywhere! They all had jolly faces—some were fishing in a pond, others pushing wheelbarrows or carrying baskets.

There were also pottery toadstools and
animals. "Oh ... wow!" said Mia.

"I collect yard ornaments," Mrs. Crooks said,
looking happy at their reaction.

Mary smiled. "Do you like them, girls?"

"Yes," said Mia, looking around in
astonishment. Sorrel had been right— there were
a lot of gnomes ... but they weren't sinister. The
yard was like a fairy-tale forest scene.

"I'd love a yard like this," said Sita.

"Jenny's been collecting since we were
children," said Mary. "Some of them are really
valuable now."

"Is that why you have such a high fence?"
Lexi asked.

Mrs. Crooks nodded. "I had a couple of
pieces stolen from the yard at my old house,
so I had the fence put up when I moved in
here." She headed up a winding gravel path.
Reaching the shed, she put her finger to her
lips and opened the door. It was dark inside,
and the air was filled with the scent of hay and
animals. There were cages, just as Mia had seen
in her mirror. Some were empty, but others had
animals in them—the girls could see that some
of them had bandages or wounds that had been
recently stitched up. The animals blinked warily
at the girls in the dim light.

"There's a squirrel," whispered Lexi.

"And rabbits and a baby badger," added
Violet.

"These animals will all be released into the
wild again soon," Mrs. Crooks said in a low
voice. "When I find an injured animal, I bring

it here first. The vet comes to assess the animals and takes the ones that need a lot of veterinary help to the sanctuary." Her face softened as she looked at them. "They're my little beauties, and I try my best to help them so they can be set free."

Mia swallowed. She suddenly realized that they'd been so, so wrong about Mrs. Crooks. She wasn't the person doing dark magic. She was just an elderly woman who loved animals.

"Jenny goes out into the woods looking for injured animals," said Mary.

"I'm sorry if I've been bad-tempered with you, girls," Mrs. Crooks said gruffly. "So many young people don't think about how their actions affect the wildlife—they leave litter, set off fireworks that scare animals, disturb their nests and habitats."

"We'd never do that," Sita said.

"I realize that now," said Mrs. Crooks. "I'm sorry. I shouldn't have been so quick to judge."

She pulled the door shut, and the girls followed her back up the path. As Mia saw the gnomes again, she thought of something. "Mrs. Crooks, did you give a gnome to the Eastons?"

"The Eastons? No, I don't know who you mean," said Mrs. Crooks.

"They live on Brook Street. There's a big trampoline in the front yard," said Mia, feeling puzzled. She'd definitely seen Mrs. Crooks with the Wish Gnome—so either the magic had been wrong, or Mrs. Crooks was lying.

Mrs. Crooks's face cleared. "Oh, I know that house. They do have a gnome in the yard, don't they? I picked it up to look at it a week or so ago when I was passing by. I couldn't resist. It was a nice specimen, and yes, just like some of mine, but no, I didn't give it to them."

Mia's breath left her in a rush. So the image she'd seen had been Mrs. Crooks admiring the gnome, but she hadn't been the person who had given it to Paige's mom. "Thank you for showing us the animals," Mia said.

"Yes, and we'll come and visit the sanctuary soon," said Sita.

"Make sure you come and find me when you do," said Mrs. Crooks, leading them through the house and letting them out the front door. "And I'll give you a guided tour."

They said good-bye, and she shut the door.

The girls looked at each other. "Okay, so maybe we got it wrong," said Lexi slowly.

They all nodded. "We really did," said Mia.

"But if Mrs. Crooks didn't conjure the Shades, who did?" said Sita.

"I still think it must be someone who knows we're Star Friends," said Violet.

Mia lifted her chin. "Well, they can try all they like, but they're not going to stop us—we're going to find out who's using dark magic."

"They've got no chance against us," Lexi said. "Not with Sita's power."

"It's *all* of our powers that will stop them," said Sita.

Lexi smiled. "The important thing is that we did it—we sent all four Shades back to the shadows."

"And next we'll deal with whoever it is using dark magic," said Mia. "Won't we?" She held her up hand.

"Definitely," they all chorused, high-fiving her.

Just then, there was a beep of a car horn, and Mrs. Greene pulled up alongside them. "Ready for some homemade pizza, girls?" she asked, and the friends all piled into the car.

Mia looked out the window at the pretty town of Westport as they drove back to her house. Together with her friends and their Star Animals, they would keep everyone safe and happy. Nothing—and no one—was going to stop them.

ABOUT THE AUTHOR

Linda Chapman is the best-selling author of more than 200 books. The biggest compliment she can have is for a child to tell her he or she became a reader after reading one of her books. She lives in a cottage with a tower in Leicestershire, England, with her husband, three children, three dogs, and three ponies. When she's not writing, Linda likes to ride, read, and visit schools and libraries to talk to people about writing.

ABOUT THE ILLUSTRATOR

Lucy Fleming has been an avid doodler and bookworm since early childhood. Drawing always seemed like so much fun, but she never dreamed it could be a full-time job! She lives and works in a small town in England with her partner and a little black cat. When not at her desk, she likes nothing more than to be outdoors in the sunshine with a cup of hot tea.